Prai...

MASTODON FARM

A NOVELLA BY
MIKE KLEINE

ATLATL

ATLATL

Dayton, Ohio

Mastodon Farm
First Edition

Copyright © Mike Kleine 2012

ISBN-13: 978-0-9849692-8-9
ISBN-10: 0984969284

Printed in the United States of America

Design by Mike Kleine
Illustrations by Austin Breed
Pixel artwork by Richard Blok

This one is for Bob, aka prince_afa

What matters in life is not what happens to you but what you remember and how you remember it.

Gabriel García Márquez

Every hundred feet, the world changes.

Roberto Bolaño, *2666*

MASTODON FARM

FERRARIS AND AFRICAN MASKS

You have a lot of money so you buy a Ferrari.

You drive the Ferrari around town for a bit.

You listen to Philip Glass.

You aren't sure which song is playing because you forgot to label the track when you uploaded it to your iPhone but you're pretty sure it's something from *Einstein on the Beach*.

You think, *God,* Einstein on the Beach *is pretty fucking amazing.*

You think about Philip Glass and his genius for a while—occasionally pressing pause on the CD player to mull over the music and imagine yourself as a character in a film from the 80s—and then you brake somewhat slowly and stop at a red light.

You sit there and wait for something to happen but then you also think about your favorite film.

Now, an abridged version of 'The Thieving Magpie' by Giacchino Rossini is playing on the Ferrari's stereo.

You are sweating because you are excited.

7

You are excited because when you listen to Philip Glass, you always see an image.

The same image.

A picture of yourself.

A movie.

You are conducting an orchestra, somewhere, in the middle of the desert.

You are dressed like James Bond.

Your orchestra is playing something good. Something like 'The Thieving Magpie'—probably.

You are wearing your favorite pair of Calvin Klein designer slacks.

You are also wearing a brand new Marc by Marc Jacobs cotton shirt, salmon.

For shoes, you have on a pair of Gucci loafers.

Nothing can surpass your sense of fashion and style.

The iPhone in your pocket vibrates.

"Yes."

"The masks," James Franco says. "They're damaged."

It's faint but you can hear it. James Franco is listening to 'Bubba Dub Bossa' by Robby Poitevin.

"Are you listening to 'Bubba Dub Bossa' by Robby Poitevin?" you ask the iPhone, confused but also relieved it is James Franco and not Ryan Gosling.

"Yes, I am listening to 'Bubba Dub Bossa' by Robby Poitevin," James Franco says, "but the masks, they're damaged," James Franco repeats into the iPhone.

"What do you mean the masks are damaged?"

"They're damaged," he says into the iPhone.

"James Franco, I'm afraid I don't understand what you are saying."

"Is the connection that bad?" he says, sounding a little bored.

"No, like, I just don't *get* what you are saying—James Franco," and you pause to take a breath, "the masks are damaged?"

"Yes—the masks—they're damaged," he says into the iPhone.

You don't say anything, not right away at least; instead, you think about the word *masks* and imagine a big neon sign.

Somewhere in the sky, there is a big neon sign and it is floating behind some clouds and it is flashing the word *masks* in bright blue letters over and over again.

And the neon sign is buzzing very loudly and flickering in a super distracting manner and the word *masks* keeps appearing—forever, in the sky.

Right next to the Ferrari, there is this young couple hanging out in a white 1980 Honda Civic hatchback.

'A-Punk' by Vampire Weekend is playing from somewhere inside the Honda and the girl in the passenger seat is nodding to the song and quietly humming to herself.

You look out the window from the driver's side of the Ferrari and onto the street and think about James Franco and his face and his body and his feet and his ears and his mouth and his words and his book, *Palo Alto*.

And then there is the slightly muted—clicking—sound of James Franco smacking his lips and you say, "Hello," and James Franco says, "yes."

You focus on the discussion about the masks.

"So the masks are damaged?" you sigh into the iPhone.

"The masks are damaged."

"Uh—when you say masks, what exactly do you mean, James Franco?"

"The masks in the box," James Franco says.

"The masks in the box?"

There is a brief silence—a lull—in the phone conversation but, already, three minutes of the abridged version of 'The Thieving Magpie' have passed and you make note of this.

"James Franco, do you realize this is probably the longest red light I have ever sat through?" you say.

"You're at a red light?" James Franco says.

"Yes, I am at a red light."

"Okay."

You stare at something on the windshield and then think about the Milky Way and other cosmic stuff.

You consider something else.

"James Franco, I don't own any masks *in a box*."

You suddenly realize the song coming from the Honda is actually 'Cousins' and not 'A-Punk'.

"Well, someone's box of African masks suddenly fell from the bookshelf this morning and now," he sighs, "they're damaged."

You hear a sound coming from the iPhone, like James Franco is moving the masks around. "And some are definitely broken, like, in pieces."

"In pieces?"

"*Pieces*," he confirms.

"Like what do you mean *pieces*, James Franco?"

"I mean pieces," he pauses. "Your masks are in pieces."

"All of them?"

"Well," and you hear noise, like James Franco is moving the masks around, again. "Yeah, most of them."

You look down at your Calvin Klein slacks and rub your left leg to make sure you are real.

"So the box fell off the bookshelf?"

"*Off* the bookshelf, yes."

"What kind of books do I read?" you ask the iPhone.

"There are no books on the bookshelf right now."

"No, what kind of books do *I* read?" you say, again.

"You don't have any books on the bookshelf," James Franco says.

"No books on the bookshelf?"

"No—just a bunch of DVDs. Like," and James Franco pauses to drink water or something, and then begins to list: "*Buckaroo Banzai, El Topo, Catfish, Encounters at the End of the World, Burn After Reading, Heat, Carnage, Cop Land, Kill List, Police Academy 7, Assault on Precinct 13, Kickboxer, Bad Boys I & II, Crash, Before the Devil Knows You're Dead, Greenberg, Blairwitch Project, Sleeping Beauty, Chinatown, Ran, The Master, The Virgin Suicides, The Breakfast Club,*

Beverly Hills Cop, Midnight Cowboy, Along Came a Spider, The International, Primer, Pi, About Schmidt, Man On Wire, The Town, Exit Through The Gift Shop, Hackers, Kazaam, Clerks 2, The Vanishing, Brick, Half Nelson, Boys Don't Cry, Outer Space, Senna, A Fish Called Wanda, Magic Mike, Cry-Baby, Dogtooth, Pink Flamingos, Four Lions, Leviathan, Boyz N The Hood, Dr. Horrible's Sing-Along Blog, Hellboy, Demolition Man, Lolita, Liquid Sky, The Birth of a Nation, a French film called *Caché, The Men Who Stare At Goats, Charlie Wilson's War, Tyrannosaur, Nude On the Moon, The Happening, Cohen and Tate, Session 9, Margin Call, I Love You Phillip Morris, The Wrestler* by Darren Aronofsky, and *Super, Contact, Hirsute, I'm Still Here, Mondo cane 1 & 2, Head, The Thirteenth Floor, Repulsion, Caravaggio, 25th Hour, The Warriors,* the original *The Taking of Pelham One Two Three, Witch Hunt, The Aviator, Michael Clayton* with George Clooney, *Escape from New York,* and then *Baghead* and Seth Rogen's *Observe and Report* and all the *Friday* movies, *Salo, Or the 120 Days of Sodom, Titanic, 2046, Enter the Void, The Kiss, Freaks, Song of the South, Caligula, Mr. Freedom, Speed Racer, Tower Heist, Sideways* with Paul Giamatti, *Eyes Wide Shut* with Nicole Kidman and Tom Cruise—that one's the Blu-ray Collector's Edition," James Franco says, "*Inland Empire, Buried, Black Moon, The Toxic Avenger, The Gods Must Be Crazy, Rope, Once Upon a Time There Was a Singing Black Bird, Rebels of the Neon God, Swan Lake: The Zone, Wild Strawberries, The Gore Gore Girls, Blacula, The Day of the Jackal, The Squid and the*

Whale, eXistenZ, Of Freaks and Men, The Hypothesis of the Stolen Painting, Killer of Sheep, The Cabinet of Dr. Caligari, The Death King and this other movie, a documentary maybe, *Koyaan*—something."

"*Koyaanisqatsi*," you say into the iPhone.

"*Koyaanisqatsi*," James Franco repeats. "And you have a bunch of other movies that are like, foreign. Untranslated."

"So was it the wind then?"

"What?"

"Did the wind knock down the masks—the box?" you say.

"The box fell on its own."

"How do you know it wasn't the wind?"

"I wasn't around when the box fell off the bookshelf this morning so I don't know for sure it was the wind—I just assume it fell on its own."

"I mean, is the window open right now?"

"I'm just guessing right now."

"James Franco, is the window open?"

A brief silence indicates James Franco is checking the window.

He gets up and says, "I'm walking over to where the window is since I can't see anything from where I am."

During this, you inspect the Honda Civic couple again and notice the girl has very small ears.

You like that the girl has very small ears.

"I just opened the window."

"Like, right now—?"

"No, I opened it a few minutes ago when I walked into the room to commence cleaning so it's already open."

"So you definitely opened the window?"

"I'm not sure."

"So you don't know."

"I don't know for sure."

Someone honks.

This startles you.

You look to your left and then to your right and then up at the light and see that it is finally green.

Now, 'Chasing Sheep is Best Left to Shepherds' from Michael Nyman and the Michael Nyman Band is playing inside the Ferrari.

Someone keeps honking.

You look into the rear-view mirror—at the car behind— and see that it is Will Smith in a metallic gray Honda Accord mouthing the words *what* and *the* and *fuck* over and over and over, and honking even more.

On the phone, James Franco says something.

"Light's green, James Franco," you breathe out. "Can't talk right now, gotta go."

"And the masks?" James Franco asks the iPhone.

You hang up and end the conversation with James Franco.

Not on purpose, of course, but because you don't want to look like a fool in front of Will Smith.

Will Smith swerves out from behind you and speeds up to the driver's side of the Ferrari and coasts and gives you the finger and yells something like, "Fuck you," probably, and speeds up again and swerves to the left and back to the right, and then zooms off into the sunset.

And you think: *Will Smith is drunk.*

You look down at the iPhone screen.

You sigh and begin to feel sorry for James Franco.

LISBON, PORTUGAL

You fly to Lisbon on a private company jet.

David Fincher directs this segment.

In Lisbon, the air is warm—no, hot.

You visit your college friend (Joan Didion).

You majored in Sociology and Mathematics.

Joan Didion majored in French.

She specializes in the sale and reproduction of African masks.

Things play out like a scene from a movie and everything is made to look like a music video.

You tell Joan Didion about the incident with the masks.

The words *African* and *masks* flash across the screen in bold white lettering.

Joan Didion seems to feel sorry.

She says something about the value of the yen and then something else about the stock market.

"That's a shame," Joan Didion says. "Really, about the masks."

"That's what I said," you say.

A speech bubble hovers above your head for a few

moments, then pops audibly and evaporates into a mess of smoke and steam.

You exchange pleasantries. This lasts a few minutes.

You eventually suggest that Joan Didion maybe visit the Grand Canyon sometime.

"You know—to enjoy yourself a little or something," you say.

A shot of the Grand Canyon: bright lights and then 'Whatever You Like' by T.I.

"We aren't in this forever," you say.

She laughs and asks something.

"Would you like to replace the African masks?"

You tell Joan Didion you would like to eventually replace the African masks—yes.

"I probably won't be able to get you the same masks," Joan Didion says.

"I don't really care about all that," you say. "I just want some African masks."

"Why do you need African masks anyway?" Joan Didion asks.

"I'm working on a project," you say.

"Why do you need African masks?" Joan Didion says, again.

"Okay, I'm not working on a project," you say.

You look at each other for a good while and—on cue—Joan Didion takes a giant sip from her iced decaf mocha latte and smiles at the camera.

You think about what you have to say.

'Tarzan Boy' by Baltimora is playing.

"I just want things to be back to normal," you say, finally. "Like how they were before."

Joan Didion nods at this and considers something else.

"I guess this has nothing to do with the masks then," she says.

THE CANYONS

In Beverly Hills, you run into Celine Dion.

The sun is out and everything looks like a video game from 1987.

It's a beautiful day, basically.

You're driving your red Ferrari and Celine Dion is sitting in the front passenger seat.

You drive back to your place and listen to 'I Think Ur A Contra' by Vampire Weekend.

Then—at her place—you talk about sushi and hi-tops and chocolate-covered fruit and probiotics and silver earrings and you go out for sushi.

An hour later, you come back to your place and talk some more, this time about Michael Jordan and winter sports and schools in France and David Foster Wallace and red wine vinegar and air filters and mustard gas and the Beatles and U2.

Then you fuck.

After that, you drink some Gran Patrón Platinum.

You watch a few scenes from *Goodfellas* and then fuck some more.

In the middle of the night, you wake up and you can't sleep anymore so you go downstairs—alone—and begin to compose this exceptional piece of music on the baby grand in the downstairs living room.

Your music wakes Celine Dion and she sits in bed for a while, at first, but then she comes downstairs.

She sits on the lime green sofa.

She listens to you play and then, she sings something to herself.

"Is that new?" you ask.

"No, it's one of my songs," she says.

You continue to play the baby grand.

You play something inspired by Philip Glass: complete with arpeggios, natural silences, accidentals and the half-way executed minimal aesthetic that makes a Philip Glass song a Philip Glass song.

As you are playing, you begin to visualize synths from the 80s and then some from the 90s. And then you think about music theory.

Celine Dion sings another song.

"Something I wrote a while back," she says.

You begin to feel sore.

PICASSO

You have lunch with this guy who says he's an astrophysicist.

"I work for NASA," he says.

He tells you his name.

"My name is Scott," he says.

Scott tells you that, "Pretty soon, NASA is going to launch a satellite probe to Venus," for something that has to do with "deep space exploration and quantum physics."

You realize you know nothing about deep space exploration—or quantum physics for that matter—so, instead, you talk to Scott about Liam Neeson and the Spice Girls.

After a while, Scott orders a Caesar salad.

You decide you aren't very hungry so you order a Perrier.

And then, sometime after lunch, you go back to a hotel room with Scott and discuss the film *2001: A Space Odyssey*, its sequel, and then you buy a Picasso.

You write out a check for $433,000

You drive the Ferrari back to your Manhattan triplex and tell James Franco you bought a Picasso.

"I just bought a Picasso," you say.

"A Picasso," James Franco says.

"A Picasso," you say. "For pretty cheap too, I think."

"Which one?" James Franco says.

"*This* one."

"The Picasso," James Franco says, pointing to the Picasso, "I've never seen it."

"Of course you've never seen it," you say, "I just bought it."

"I know," James Franco says, "but, I've never seen *that* Picasso before."

"Okay," you say.

"There's a message on the answering machine," James Franco says.

"Thanks."

You check the message.

It's Barry.

Barry's voice says something about meeting some rapper about a painting.

You think about the Picasso you just bought.

You call Barry.

"I bought a Picasso," you say.

"Come to my house," Barry says. "In like, an hour."

You wait maybe thirty minutes.

Then you drive to Barry's house.

On the way up, you listen to 'The Mollusk' by Ween and then you call Barry to tell him you are coming.

"I'm on my way," you say to the iPhone.

You talk about the rapper for a bit.

Barry tells you his music is great.

Twenty minutes later, at Barry's apartment, he admits that he really likes this rapper and wants to buy a painting from him.

"A painting?" you say.

"Yeah, something he painted," Barry says.

"I thought we were maybe going to buy a Picasso from him," you say. "Not something *he* painted."

"Does it really matter?" Barry asks. "And why would we buy a Picasso?"

You don't say anything.

Barry talks some more about the issue.

Then, a few minutes pass and he convinces you.

"You should come with me."

"And do what?" you say.

"Keep me company, I don't know," Barry says.

He offers to drive.

You agree.

Together, you leave in Barry's 2003 Rolls-Royce Silver Seraph.

At first, you listen to something by Weezer.

LIL JABBA

Then you listen to something by Henri Mancini, followed by Tangerine Dream.

Barry tells you to stop changing the songs.

"Just leave it on for like, more than a minute guy," Barry says.

"Stop telling me what to do," you say.

Barry tells you Lil Jabba is actually a producer and not a rapper.

"Lil Jabba produces footwork music," Barry explains. "It's like, from Chicago."

"What's footwork music?" you ask.

"It's this type of dance," Barry says, "you'll see."

"I thought we were going to Seattle," you say.

"We are going to Seattle."

•••

A couple of hours later, you are in Seattle.

Lil Jabba lives with his sister, in a mansion.

And Lil Jabba is white.

You thought that maybe Lil Jabba might be a black footwork music producer, but he's not.

You walk the length of the mansion, twice, while Lil Jabba talks about the paintings.

His work, the paintings—everything is scattered.

"So you don't have a room for your work? The paintings?" Barry says to Lil Jabba.

"I kind of do everything everywhere," Lil Jabba says.

"Right," Barry says.

You realize the mansion is more of a manor.

Big-house-on-top-of-the-hill type of thing.

'Sweet Jane' by The Velvet Underground is playing from somewhere.

And Lil Jabba continues with the tour.

"Yeah, so I paint these big mythical scenes, like— mythical characters in oil—generally at least six feet tall, like us, you know, and it's really what I envision my life to be beyond this thin veil of reality, I just paint what really sticks with me, down to my core."

Lil Jabba walks down the cavernous hallway, pointing to a bunch of canvases and prints—his *big mythical scenes* apparently.

"Most recently I've been working on a painting of a bunch of goons all huddled around a glowing map," he points to a painting, "some freaky cave-dwellers surrounding a camp fire," two different versions, all sitting in one corner of the room, "a Conquistador, a man lazing on a steamy beach in a hammock, two French revolutionaries circa 1795 wearing Chicago starter jackets in a sewer— huddled around a legless Creature from the Black Lagoon, my family dog George, ogre heads, my friend Clara sitting in a very sinister chair, two soldiers looking off a cliff into a foggy sunset, a group of spelunkers exiting a cave, and a footwork battle."

"See the footwork battle?" Barry says.

"I see the footwork battle," you say.

Barry buys the painting.

He writes a check for $899,998.

"And makes sure it says Alexander Shaw," Lil Jabba says.

"Who's Alexander Shaw?" you say.

"I'm Alexander Shaw," Lil Jabba says.

"He's Alexander Shaw," Barry says.

"You're Alexander Shaw," you say, to Lil Jabba.

"I'm Alexander Shaw," Lil Jabba says, with his arms out—smiling.

It's this great big grin, like something out of a movie.

CASINO ROYALE & MELROSE PLACE

At the hotel, you can't sleep.

You turn on the television.

Re-runs of *Fear Factor*.

Joe Rogan looks slim.

You get up and masturbate onto one of Barry's Louis Vuitton valises.

You look at the television, again, then at Barry—he's sleeping—and then at the television, again.

Tim Allen.

Tool Time.

You look up famous television cliffhanger endings on Wikipedia.

You click on *Melrose Place* and read some things about Kimberly Shaw and a few of the other characters.

You think about confusing films. Like *Casino Royale* with Daniel Craig.

You don't know if it's supposed to be a remake of the original, a reboot or maybe, something else.

Also, you aren't entirely sure if the film is supposed to be set in the 60s—like the original film—or present-day whatever.

And because the men are dressed in tuxedos during most of the film, it's nearly impossible to guess a decade for whenever the film is supposed to take place.

You read about *Casino Royale* for another five minutes and then, you become bored of everything.

You find your Walkman and listen to some Steve Hauschildt.

Then you fall asleep.

DEAN CAIN'S BOOKS

Dean Cain calls sometime before noon.

"I'm having a release party for a new book in my Manhattan high-rise sometime around eight this evening," Dean Cain says, "if you're interested."

"I'm interested," you say, "definitely."

You pass the time by watching a film: *Angel Heart*.

Then you watch *Palindromes*.

And then half of *The Darjeeling Limited*.

After that, you nap.

You wake up and it's a little after eight.

You drive up to Dean Cain's apartment.

At the apartment, 'Since I Left You' by The Avalanches is playing.

You notice the walls.

They are very white.

"Your walls are very white" you say.

"My walls are very white," Dean Cain says. He looks around, at his walls. And then, "My walls *are* very white," he says, again.

You notice other things.

The large and rigid rectangular French-style windows, the two crystal chandeliers, the assorted paintings, a rather odd assemblage of decanters and carafes—off to one side of the room—an antiquated liquor cabinet and several Ikea bookshelves very *very* full of books.

Books like: *The Great Gatsby* by F. Scott Fitzgerald and *Wuthering Heights* by Emily Brontë and *American Psycho* by Bret Easton Ellis and *Brand New Cherry Flavor* by Todd Grimson and *Women* by Charles Bukowski and *The Gargoyle* by Andrew Davidson and *My Uncle Oswald* by Roald Dahl and *Rant* by Chuck Palahniuk and *In Cold Blood* by Truman Capote and *One Hundred Years of Solitude* by Gabriel García-Márquez and *The Magicians* by Lev Grossman and *Caleb Williams* by William Godwin and *Things Fall Apart* by Chinua Achebe and *Mademoiselle De Scudéry And The Carte De Tendre* by James Munro and *The Picture of Dorian Gray* by Oscar Wilde and *The Corrections* by Jonathan Franzen and *Love in Excess* by Eliza Haywood and *Mr. Fox* by Helen Oyemi and *The Demon Princes* by Jack Vance and *Airships* by Barry Hannah and *Carte Blanche* by Carlo Lucarelli and *Ether* by Ben Ehrenreich and *Beyond Apollo* by Barry N. Malzberg and *China Mountain Zhang* by Maureen F. Mchugh and *The Tower* by Richard Martin Stern and *The Dog Stars* by Peter Heller and *Why Are You Doing This?* by Jason and *The Blind Assassin* by Margaret Atwood and *The Mezzanine* by Nicholson Baker and *Burr* by Gore Vidal and *Almost Transparent Blue* by Ryū Murakami and *Ubik* by Philip K. Dick and *Mr. Fortune's Maggot* by Sylvia

Townsend Warner and *Savages* by Don Winslow and *Drama City* by George Pelecanos and *The Hawkline Monster* by Richard Brautigan and *Mountains of the Moon* by I.J. Kay and *From the Observatory* by Julio Cortázar and *Guadalajara* by Quim Monzó and *The Tunnel* by William H. Gass and *Lizard Music* by Daniel Pinkwater and *The Death of the Author* by Gilbert Adair and *The Tenant* by Roland Topor and *The Carpet People* by Terry Pratchett and *Action, Figure* by Frank Hinton and *FENCES* by Ben Brooks and *Voodoo River* by Robert Crais and *Black Hole* by Charles Burns and *I Am Not Sidney Poitier* by Percival Everett and *Mr. Penumbra's 24-Hour Bookstore* by Robin Sloan and *Rubicon Beach* by Steve Erickson and T*he Hundred Brothers* by Donald Antrim and *The Third Policeman* by Flann O'Brien and *The Jungle* by Upton Sinclair and *Watch Out* by Joseph Suglia and *The Pillowman* by Martin McDonagh and *Me Talk Pretty One Day* by David Sedaris and *The Lake* by Banana Yoshimoto and *Interstellar Pig* by William Sleator and *Flatland* by Edwin A. Abbott and *Mother's Milk* by Edward St. Aubyn and *Cosmopolis* by Don DeLillo and *The Crying of Lot 49* by Thomas Pynchon and *The Old Man and the Sea* by Ernest Hemingway and *You Deserve Nothing* by Alexander Maksik and two novellas: *The Secret History of the Lord of Musashi* and *Arrowfoot* by Jun'ichirō Tanizaki and *The Wind-Up Bird Chronicle* by Haruki Murakami and *Propeller Island* by Jules Verne and *Never Let Me Go* by Kazuo Ishiguro and *Kamby Bolongo Mean River* by Robert Lopez and *The Magus* by John Fowles and *Magnetic Field* by

Ron Loewinsohn and *Creamy Bullets* by Kevin Sampsell and *Cosmos* by Witold Gombrowicz and *Hoodtown* by Christa Faust and *The Stranger* by Albert Camus and *Light Years* by James Salter and *The Mirage* by Matt Ruff and *Goliath* by Tom Gauld and *Third Class Superhero* by Charles Yu and *Feed* by M.T. Anderson and *A Monster Calls* by Patrick Ness and *Froth on the Daydream* by Boris Vian and—

"I moved here shortly after 9/11," Dean Cain says.

"Oh yeah," you say—still examining the books on the shelves

Something outside the apartment makes the sound of fire crackers and Dean Cain walks over to the window to see what is happening.

You spot *Palo Alto*.

"Kids," Dean Cain says.

You repeat the word.

"Kids."

'Lalibela' by Caribou is playing.

JAI ALAI

You feel terrible.

You go to a Knicks game.

Jack Nicholson is there. You sit by him.

You say something and Jack Nicholson looks at you and smiles. He doesn't even say, "Hello."

He probably doesn't realize it's you.

Whatever.

You don't understand the game.

The rules don't make sense.

You don't recognize any of the players.

In the neighborhood where you grew up, people only ever played polo, tennis, lacrosse, squash and jai alai.

At half-time, you look up at the scoreboard.

The Knicks are losing by fifteen points.

ACCIDENT

You are driving home.

You listen to 'Untrust Us' by Crystal Castles.

Someone side-swipes the Ferrari.

You almost strike three pedestrians and crash into a Dunkin' Donuts.

This is somewhere near the Brooklyn Bridge and you find out—later—the lady who hit you, she died.

She was old.

"Wasn't wearing her glasses," someone on the street says.

"She was basically driving blind," the police officer says. "I'm surprised this didn't happen earlier."

An EMT examines you.

You try and act normal.

"Am I hurt?" you ask.

"You're not hurt," the EMT says.

You talk to the cops.

"Am I in trouble?" you ask.

"You're not in trouble," a young cop says.

You freak out a little.

You can smell pomade in your sweat.

"Everything is under control," someone says—another police officer.

You freak out some more.

•••

Later, they let you go home, but the insurance company wants to figure things out.

"The insurance company wants to figure things out," you say to James Franco. "Can you talk to them?"

"I can talk to them," James Franco says.

You go to bed and James Franco calls the insurance company.

•••

An hour later.

"They took the Ferrari to Joe's Body Shop," James Franco says. "It's going to take maybe three weeks to get everything back to how it was."

"I just want things to be back to normal," you say. "Like how they were before."

James Franco tells you that the parts for the Ferrari need to be shipped in from New Zealand, so it may take longer than expected.

"Like how long?" you say.

"I don't know, an extra week maybe," James Franco says.

"What am I going to drive?"

"We'll figure that out tomorrow."

CHAMPAGNE

You go with James Franco to the car place.

You look at some cars for an hour and decide to buy a Bentley Mulsanne.

Built-in AM tuner.

"Champagne," the car salesman says.

You turn on the radio.

"I'm sorry, what?" James Franco says.

"Champagne," the car salesman says again. "That's the color of the car—the name. Champagne. Super popular with the kids these days."

You tell the car salesman you are not a kid.

"I'm not a kid," you say.

Justin Bieber is singing from inside one of the cars.

The salesman touches your arm and laughs about something.

CONCUSSIONS

You call your father.

You tell him about the accident with the Ferrari.

Then you tell him about the Bentley.

"It's a Mulsanne," you say.

You call your mother.

You tell her about the old lady who died and the color of the car and the cops and the insurance people and James Franco.

"It wasn't my fault," you say.

You tell her it's going to take four weeks—maybe five to fix the Ferrari.

"They have to order parts from like, New Zealand or something, I think," you say.

You tell her you are glad to be okay.

And then later, you call your father again.

You tell him about the Bentley.

"I'm sorry dad, I already told you about all this," you say.

"It's alright," he says. "Maybe you have a concussion. Did you go see the doctor about a concussion?"

"I don't have a concussion," you say. "I didn't go see a

doctor."

"You didn't go see a doctor?"

"No, just an EMT," you say.

"Just an EMT?" he says.

"The EMT came to me, actually," you say. "Like right after the accident."

"And the EMT didn't say anything about a concussion?"

"No, the EMT said nothing about a concussion, dad."

"Well, be careful," he says. "I hear you aren't supposed to sleep right away—after a concussion."

ASHTON KUTCHER'S HOUSE

You drive to Ashton Kutcher's house in the champagne Bentley Mulsanne—with the built-in AM tuner—and you listen to 'Emergency Room' by Ford & Lopatin then, 'Where I Belong' by DVA, followed by 'Blue Dream' by Hype Williams.

You drive around for a bit and realize—after a little while—that you are lost and probably have no idea where Ashton Kutcher lives. Also, you don't know where you are going, but you don't feel like stopping at a gas station to ask for directions (and you think someone working a gas station probably has no business knowing where Ashton Kutcher lives anyway) so you drive around some more.

An hour passes.

Now, 'Commissioning a Symphony in C' by Cake is playing.

You realize you've never actually been to Ashton Kutcher's house.

Sure, you've been invited dozens of times but you've

never actually been to Ashton Kutcher's house. You sent a postcard, once, from Lisbon, for his birthday, but you've never actually been to Ashton Kutcher's house.

You call James Franco.

"I'm lost," you say into the iPhone.

James Franco says something about a bowling alley and an hour later, you meet at a pizzeria.

Together, you go to a screening of a new Ryan Gosling film.

KINGS AND THINGS

At another party, after the screening of the new Ryan Gosling film, three people are standing around and talking about the new Steven Spielberg film.

A copy of *Palo Alto* is sitting on a coffee table in one of the living rooms.

The 'Jamie xx Rework Part 3' of the Radiohead song 'Bloom' is playing and Edward Norton is talking about how he has problems with contact lenses.

He says his eyes get irritated and turn super red.

"And I'm not allergic to anything," he says. "That's what's so weird."

Someone's dog is here.

A St. Bernard.

You notice the dog is standing—sitting next to a woman.

A girl, actually.

A very plain-looking girl.

And she's admiring paintings on the wall.

You find her to be very boring-looking, in addition to being very plain-looking.

You hear voices coming from somewhere and you look.

Four people are sitting on some couches in the third living room.

They are eating caviar and talking loudly.

They are also playing a game.

One of them, a black man, has a piece of paper stuck to his forehead.

The word *Godzilla* is written in big block letters.

"Am I like, from the 80s?" he says.

"You *can* be," a girl says.

"Yes or no answers only," the other girl says. Asian.

The first girl, the one who said, "You *can* be," she also has a card on her forehead. Her card says *Donald Trump*, and this is written in blue ink—like from a fountain pen.

The second guy, his card says *Don Cheadle*. He's not black though, like the other guy. French, maybe.

"Is it my turn now?" he says, with the accent.

"Not yet," the first girl says.

That accent. It's his voice you like best, you decide.

The second girl, the one who didn't say, "You *can* be," but, "yes or no answers only," you can't see her card right away but she laughs about something and then turns your way, for a few seconds—long enough for you to read her card—and then turns back to the people playing the game and asks something.

Something about being dead.

You think about her card and laugh out loud.

FRIENDS

You drive to Matthew Perry's house.

It's early evening but you aren't too sure of the exact time.

In fact, you are never too sure of the time.

You listen to 'Betrayed in the Octagon' by Oneohtrix Point Never.

At the house, there's Matthew Perry, Courtney Cox and David Arquette.

They talk about one of the Scream movies.

You talk about Wes Anderson.

David Arquette mentions something about Francis Ford Coppola and then Matthew Perry talks about *Madagascar*, you aren't really sure which one though.

Courtney Cox reveals that they—Jennifer Aniston, Matt LeBlanc, Lisa Kudrow, David Schwimmer and Matthew Perry—have all been talking about maybe doing a *Friends* film.

"I like that idea," you say. "Really, I think it's fresh."

THE GREAT GREAT GATSBY

Outside: something resembling Godzilla attacks the city.

At the party, 'Faith' by George Michael is playing and someone is telling you to consider changing apartments.

Move to the Upper East Side.

"I like my apartment too much," you say, "it's a triplex."

She ignores your comment and says she knows someone who could easily lease this really great flat for pretty cheap.

"Like, around three-grand a month," she says with something that sounds almost like a South African accent.

You feel like she is trying to sell you something you really don't need.

Someone else—an older gentleman—says something about a guy named Brandon.

"I think you mean Barry," you say.

"No, I mean Brandon," he says.

And then this woman you met once at a convention in Minneapolis (by accident) waves.

She walks over.

She talks about her problems and how she can't seem to get through to her son because he now lives in Lisbon and she doesn't know whether he still has feelings for this guy, Ryan, and that her last book—nonfiction on the current state of music—didn't sell too well.

She continues with her story.

Like how now she is having issues with the publisher on this next project of hers.

"I'm writing about *Ivy league Music*," she says.

You feel like you really don't care about what she has to say.

You excuse yourself and order a Kir Royale.

'Something For Cat' by Henri Mancini & His Orchestra is playing.

A pretty girl with blond hair and green eyes is standing by a very tall man.

She smiles at you from across the room

You look somewhere else.

Something distracts her because she bumps into a table and falls back onto the tall man.

This surprises him.

She drops her wine glass onto the persimmon rug—ruining it, forever—and then covers her mouth and giggles a little and mouths, "Shit."

She looks up at the tall man and smiles and then looks back at you.

She looks embarrassed, a little.

You want to tell her that if the tall man standing next to

her is her boyfriend, she ought to dump him—probably—because truthfully, he isn't that good looking.

But really—and this, because you are weak—you just watch her leave the room with the tall man.

That's all you do.

Outside: the sky turns a weird shade of purple and great big gobs of cum smack the pavement—scenes from an experimental film: the early 90s.

At the party, you recognize: Aron, Christian, Tyrone, Marques, Evian, Ashlie, Denise, Ruth, Joel, Shandi, Bill, Jarod, Powell, Temple, Monique, Tamique, Curt, Juliette, Malcolm, Glen, E. Cuthbert Williams (Willy), Debra, Jeanne, Jona, Alice, Griffin III, Yan, Hilary, Augustus, Georges, Chadwick, Zaïda, Manuel, Al, Everett, Millie, Keith, Loren, Robert, Ernst, Rev. Bill Ramus, Paul, Jude, Riff, Kenneth, Caryl, Viola, Julianne, Carlos, Merriweather, Roy, Dick, T-Barrr, Alton, Donn, Bradley, Mao Mao, Delma, Milan, Quinn, Edward, Werner, Gwen, Hems Jr, Samuel, Sydney, Danica, Marion, Alan, K. K. Smith, Molly, Inida, Eggie, Shelton, Lucien, Gus, Garth, Larry, Patricia, Laural, Jupiter, Bertha, Sherice, Dr. Daniel Gregory Oswald (Dr. DGO), Tito, Patsy, Kendrick, Freeman, Gabrìel, Beverley, Fritz, Lottie, Teddy Hoover, Arlean, Lesha, Dorina, Dusty, Jesse, Walt, Jackson, Ivan, Twyla, Minerva, Nora, Diego, Lee Lee, Mac, Carf, Peter (Marques' shrink), Taylor and Tyler, Buffer (a producer of electronic music), Seth, Desmond (or Dezzy), Diggins (some sort of exec), Scott (the astrophysicist from the other day), a few super models, a magician, Nora, three waiters, a bartender, Silvestre and James Franco—who is playing DJ.

Then there are about twelve other people you don't recognize.

Something in your pocket vibrates.

A text message: *Fuck you, fuck you—I hope you die!*

You scan the room, to see if anyone is maybe holding a cell phone or looking at you funny.

It takes a minute.

But no one looks like they could have written the message: *fuck you, fuck you—I hope you die!*

Sebastian Tellier is on the stereo: 'Manty'

•••

An hour passes and suddenly, it's nine-thirty

You begin to feel tired.

You see this girl. She looks attractive enough and she has dark hair and big brown eyes so you decide to have a conversation.

P.T. Anderson does this part.

"Do you remember me? I think we've met before," you say.

"Do I remember you?" she says.

"Yeah, I think it was at some party last month."

"A party last month?"

"Yeah, a party last month," you say. "I'm pretty sure it was a party last month."

"What did we talk about?" she asks. "At the party last month."

"Music I think."

"Music?"

"Yeah, music."

She rolls her eyes at you.

Then she smiles.

"I want you to actually teach me how to read music this time," you say.

"How to read music," she says.

"Yeah, so I can maybe learn how to read while I'm playing, or something."

"And this is what we were talking about last time?" she says. "You're sure?"

"I am absolutely sure," you say, this time with a tone, pretending to be serious. "Totally."

"Totally?"

"Yeah, totally," you say, again, still with the same tone, pretending to be serious, still.

She likes it.

"I thought you said you already knew how to read music," she says, finally, playing along. "Last time we spoke."

"Well I can't. Remember? I just memorize everything," you say. "I don't really know how to play music."

"That's a shame," she says. "You just have to practice. Besides, you look like you maybe know how to read music already."

"I don't know what that means," you say, "but you're like, classically trained or something, I think, you said that last time. I learned by watching videos on the internet and stuff."

"No you didn't," she says.

"Sure I did."

Across the room, Georges makes eye contact.

You wave.

"Your friend is very rude," she says.

"Why is that?"

"He didn't wave back."

"He's busy."

"You're busy."

"Oh yeah?" you say.

You look her up and down.

She's definitely enjoying this.

"You know, my friends have been telling me stories about you. Like how you're actually someone super-famous."

"*Someone* super-famous?" she repeats.

"Super-famous," you say. "Like ridiculous-famous."

"Ridiculous-famous," she says this time, with a smile. "But you," and she touches your arm with her hand, "I hear you're not nice to girls."

"I don't really know about all that," you say, acting like she just said something in a language you don't understand.

"You *are* kind of mean," someone says.

You turn around and see a man you have never seen before.

You make a face that looks surprised.

Though really, you are surprised—a little.

He is acting like he knows you.

But then, he says something else.

"I'm just playing."

And she laughs as he walks away.

"Do you know him?" she says with a smile.

You shrug and make a face like you don't know.

You even forget what the man looks like after a few seconds.

•••

Half an hour passes.

Tyrone walks in and says something.

This is distracting so you stop talking.

You turn and look at Tyrone.

Tyrone is smiling and holding what looks like a very expensive ceremonial sword.

"Look, everyone, I'm Kill Bill," he says.

He begins to mock-dance with the sword in his hands.

Tyrone sways his hips back and forth.

He is beginning to sweat.

People start to laugh—even Taylor and Evian and Zaïda and Edward and Tito and Danica and Millie and a few other attractive girls you couldn't recognize—except for Marques who, for some reason, looks pissed off.

"This, ladies and gentleman, is a Korean katana," Tyrone declares.

Tyrone is lying to everyone—but also, he isn't really—because he doesn't actually know that what he thinks is a Korean katana is actually an expensive ceremonial sword, not from Korea.

"Where did you get that?" someone yells and then, a series of laughs.

"Remember Leonardo from the Ninja Turtles?" Tyrone says, again, speaking to no one in particular.

He slices the air with the sword.

A voice yells something else and more people laugh, together this time.

The stereo is playing something by Clive Tanaka.

Tyrone is obviously drunk and starting to get super sweaty from all the dancing he is doing.

It's disgusting.

"I'm Tom Cruise."

He begins to make swishing sounds with his mouth and says some stuff to no one in particular.

Then he pretends he is speaking Japanese.

"I'm The Last Asian," he says.

The music is fairly loud now so the scene isn't as dramatic as it should—no, could be.

A few people in the back are still talking, like they haven't even noticed Tyrone, or everything he is doing.

The girl—who is maybe someone super-famous—is now talking with someone else.

She notices that you are watching and looks back at you—briefly—and then smiles.

Outside: something falls from the sky and bursts into flames and one of the limo drivers is caught in the blast—but no one notices.

The music is pretty loud.

You begin to ignore Tyrone but then someone in the room next door laughs at something else and says, "Oh shit."

After a while, Tyrone drops the sword—like it's too heavy—and puts his hand over his mouth.

"Now I'm bored," he says with a hiccup. "I need to go punch a tree."

•••

Later, a girl with red hair says, "Don't fucking touch me."

Marques is trying to touch her so she will move away from the expensive Fred Ponset painting on the wall.

The girl you were talking to—super-famous chick—you don't see her anymore; she's gone, probably.

The girl with the red hair though, her hand bumps against the big brass frame.

She steps back, away from Marques.

Marques pushes her out of the way so he can stop the painting from falling and says, "Fuck."

The painting: it's something from Ponset's experimental phase.

Kids.

They're standing, in a semi-circle.

They're holding flint lock pistols—or guns that look like flint lock pistols.

They're wearing cowboy hats and cowboy boots.

They're shouting at each other and they're shooting the flint lock pistols at what looks like a giant black circle—or a hole, perhaps.

The circle covers a good two-thirds of the painting.

You can read the plaque: *Omega Point*.

"Cost three-hundred grand," Marques once said, "and then some change."

Marques owns the two other Ponset paintings from this same set, also—*Cosmology* and *Quantum Suicide*—all similar to this one, actually.

One in a condo somewhere in Florida and the other, in a triplex. Somewhere in London.

You've already seen the one in Miami, twice.

Outside: something makes a loud sound.

Tyrone returns from somewhere, sweatier now.

He looks at your face and says, "Hiya."

Someone—probably James Franco—puts on a track by Tennis: 'Marathon'.

"Beneath my apartment, there's like this nest made of newspaper scraps," someone says.

And then someone else says, "Oh shit," again.

The girl with the green eyes, she's texting someone when she spills her drink onto the carpet, a second time.

Something blue.

Again, you hear Marques say, "Fuck."

THE GATEKEEPER

At the apartment, Barry introduces the character of Clive.

"This is Clive," Barry says.

You look at Clive.

Clive is tall and he is very blond. Even his eyebrows.

Sort of looks like the Ken doll too—in a weird super glossy and ultra fake sort of way—you decide.

You ask a question.

"Clyde, what do you do?"

"Clive," Clive says.

"I'm sorry, what?" you say.

"His name is Clive," Barry says. "You said Clyde."

"I did?" you say.

"Yes," Barry says.

"Well I apologize, Clive. I certainly did not mean anything by that. Clive," you say.

"It's fine," Clive says.

"He says it's fine," you say to Barry.

"I heard," Barry says.

"I'm a gatekeeper," Clive says.

"A gatekeeper?" you say.

"Yeah, a gatekeeper," Barry says.

"What does that mean?" you say to Clive. And then, "A gatekeeper?" to Barry.

"He's a gatekeeper," and then to you, "for George Lucas," Barry says.

"Cool. Like a guard," you say to Barry.

"No, like a gatekeeper," Barry says to Clive.

"Yes, like a gatekeeper," Clive says to Barry.

"I'm afraid I don't follow," you say to the room.

"I'm a gatekeeper for the George Lucas Ranch."

"What is the George Lucas Ranch?" you say.

"Um—it's actually called the Skywalker Ranch, technically. It's in Marin County."

"Marin County," Barry says.

"Marin County," you say, also.

"Bill lives out in Marin County," Barry says to you.

"Yeah."

"It's Luke's office."

"So you guard the stuff?"

"Well, I never actually see the stuff," Clive says. "I'm like, literally the gatekeeper."

"He's the gatekeeper," Barry says to you.

"I work at the gate," Clive says. "I let people in."

"He lets people in," Barry says to Clive.

You think about this.

"I'm also a moderator for the unofficial Star Wars Fan Club Association forum," Clive says.

"He's one of the moderators," Barry says to the room.

PELICAN BAY

Pelican Bay with Barry.

You are sitting in someone else's living room—this guy Eric, his apartment, maybe.

You ask Barry about Eric.

"I'm not really sure who he is, really," Barry admits.

"So why are we here?"

"Business stuff," Barry says matter-of-factly.

You look at the screen on your iPhone.

You look to see what time it is but then, you forget the time, just as quickly.

Barry says something about high ceilings and white walls.

"I love a good coffee table book," Barry says. "Especially that Ernest Spelling one."

There's a book on the coffee table: *The Coffee Table Andy Warhol Picture Book.*

Barry is mildly impressed by the Andy Staton painting on the wall and says something like, "This one actually looks like it might be an *original* original, you know?"

You nod.

A silence in the air, something like electricity. You can

feel it because music was playing before and now, it's not.

For this part, things start to play like a scene from a movie—a sequel.

The new music is coming from somewhere in the apartment.

Something like 'Air on a G String' but with synthesizers—like Wendy Carlos.

The music sounds like a soundtrack.

Also, you notice the pair of massive Trenner & Friedl Duke speakers off to one corner of the room—*something like two-hundred grand*, you imagine—sitting atop a recently-varnished teak Vespucci armoire; but the music isn't coming from the speakers. No.

Somewhere else.

Eric finally enters the room, from the left side, before you can figure out where the music is coming from.

And you lose your train of thought.

He says something about some new shoes, an electronic music artist from Rhode Island and an art symposium in Orlando.

Barry looks at Eric and says something.

Then, laughter.

Eric carries most of the conversation.

A new song plays.

Schubert's 'Impromptu in G-Flat Major Opus 90 No. 3'.

You listen, sort of.

Barry is flipping through the Andy Warhol picture book.

"I really like this book, a lot," Barry says, about half a

dozen times.

There are people in the neighboring room.

They are laughing about something.

Barry licks his finger and turns a page from the book.

The Schubert piece is about to reach its climax.

"I've always wanted this book," Barry says.

More laughter.

"Don't lick your fingers," Eric says.

And then, silence, again—something like even more electricity in the air.

"I said don't lick your goddamn fingers."

V/H/S

You drive to the video rental store.

The radio is playing something foreign.

European: a dark beat.

Some sort of techno.

It's good but you switch it off and play Philip Glass.

On the highway, you see there is a sale.

The entire *Aliens* trilogy.

It's written on a billboard.

In great big white letters.

The entire set, by Ridley Scott.

$45.99 it reads.

The sale continues: "Includes *Aliens 4*," and then, "as a bonus."

This part of the ad confuses you.

What is the purpose of the sale if the word *trilogy* is written at the top?

You think about this while Philip Glass does his thing.

You realize, the set can no longer be considered a trilogy if a fourth film is added to the equation.

You think about this for a while longer.

Then you think about the film, *Casino Royale*, again.

You lose your train of thought.

You arrive at the video rental store.

There's a sign that reads: "We have every VHS—ever."

A Fiona Apple song is playing.

You browse by yourself and no one bothers you.

First, you go to the Steven Spielberg section and spend two hours looking at everything.

Then, you go to the Ben Stiller section—twice—and pick up *Tropic Thunder* the first time and then *Zoolander* the second.

You waltz over to the Lars Von Trier section.

You begin to search for *Breaking the Waves*.

You remember: *Winona Ryder is a big fan.*

You feel like you owe it to her to watch *Breaking the Waves*.

All you can find in the Lars Von Trier section is *Dogville* and *Anti-Christ* and *Dancer in the Dark* and, for some reason, *Donnie Darko*.

You find this to be mildly disappointing and extremely unsettling.

You mosey over to the checkout counter.

The clerk is wearing a neon orange jumpsuit.

The name 'Owen' is written in big block letters above the left breast pocket.

You ask Owen if it would be possible to order the film *Breaking the Waves*.

"Owen, would it be possible to have *Breaking the Waves*

delivered to my home address?" you say. "And before the end of the week, preferably."

"You're the third person to ask me that today brother," Owen says.

He's chewing gum.

"Really?" you say. "I'm the third person to ask you about *Breaking the Waves* today?"

Spearmint.

"Yeah brother man, that's what I'm telling you," Owen says.

It's quite understandable—that a film like *Breaking the Waves* would be in such high demand—actually.

"Brother, we actually have dozens of stores throughout the whole country man. We're a chain. I bet you didn't know that," Owen says. "You could probably find the film online and order it straight to your house."

You think about this for a moment.

Then you think, *I just want things to be like they were before.*

"And we can send any film to your house—and get this brother man, if the total cost exceeds $14.99, then shipping's on us!" Owen exclaims.

"That's excellent," you say, "but I have money."

"You bet it is—excellent," Owen says, and then, "good for you brother."

"Can you go check?" you say. "Like in the back, to see if you maybe don't have an extra copy of *Breaking the Waves* sitting around?"

"I can assure you brother," Owen says, "that if we had a copy of *Breaking the Waves*, then it would tell me right here on this computer."

He taps a few keys on the computer, as if to show you the computer really exists. That it does in fact make the sound of a keyboard tapped by fingers.

"Thanks but I'd really like it if you checked," you insist, "for *Breaking the Waves*."

Owen looks at you.

"Please."

"Sure brother," he says. "Just wait right here."

You wait three minutes.

You look around and notice that the video store also has an Uma Thurman section.

Owen returns.

"Sorry brother," Owen says, "we don't have an extra copy of *Breaking the Waves* sitting around."

A moment passes.

And you ask, "Do you have *Casino Royale*?"

UMA THURMAN WEARS SPANX

You aren't very hungry so you drink a martini (stirred) and then eat the olive.

You call Uma Thurman.

You tell her about the Picasso.

"$433,000," you say. "Do you think that's a good—a fair price?"

"I guess," Uma Thurman says.

You also tell her about the Uma Thurman section at the video store.

She sounds surprised but you can tell she is play-acting, for you.

She probably already knew about the Uma Thurman section at the video store.

Just like James Franco knows there's a James Franco section at the video store in Petaluma.

You talk about the color green, lemon trees, pencil sharpeners, iPads, the 100-most influential people article in

Time magazine, Mike Tyson, Tracy Chapman, Bob Marley, Quentin Tarantino, Tracy Morgan and Skittles.

You yawn into the phone and Uma Thurman hears that you are yawning.

"Is that you yawning?" she asks.

"That's me yawning," you say.

"I thought that might be you yawning," she says.

You tell Uma Thurman you are maybe thinking about going to France for a few weeks. "To clear my mind," you say.

"To clear your mind," she says, "that's good."

She tells you the last time she saw you, you looked good—"Tired but good."

"It was like you hadn't slept or something."

"I probably didn't—hadn't," you say.

"Don't go to South America though," she says.

"Okay, I won't," you say. "Why?"

She ignores the question.

You tell Uma Thurman you're also thinking about maybe opening a separate checking account with American Express and that you want to order the gold edition of the card because you are tired of the platinum version, the way it looks mostly.

Uma Thurman yawns into the phone.

You hear that she is yawning.

"Are you yawning like that on purpose?" you say.

"No," she says.

"Okay," you say.

"Is there something you want for your birthday?" she says.

"My birthday already happened."

"I mean, for like, your *next* year birthday," she says, "something special, maybe."

You answer immediately.

"I want *Breaking the Waves*, by Lars Von Trier," you say.

"Don't you already have that?" she says.

"No, I don't already have that," you say.

"Well maybe I already have that."

"You may."

"Well—I'm sure I'll think of something," she says.

You don't say anything.

Silence.

After a bit, Uma Thurman says, "Good night" and you say, "yeah" and together, you hang up almost at the same time but really, Uma Thurman is first to put down the phone.

THE MAGIC HOUR AT LAKE MEAD

You drive the Bentley to Lake Mead.

It's afternoon, you think.

You listen to a bootleg cassette audio book of *Ms. Hempel Chronicles* by Sarah Shun-lien Bynum.

James Franco is narrating.

Allen sends you a text.

Text me when ur here.

•••

Im here.

You park the car near a red Chevy Malibu.

Allen is wearing a Cardinals hat and khaki shorts.

"Is this your first time," he says, "to Lake Mead?"

"Yes," you say.

He hands you a beer.

"What do you think?" Allen says.

"I like beer."

"No, the lake," Allen says, and he points at the lake with his free hand.

"It's nice," you say. "*Lake Mead*."

"Why are you saying it like that?" Allen says. "*Lake Mead*."

And then he laughs.

"I don't know what you mean."

Allen laughs some more.

"We never think about that stuff though, do we?" Allen says.

"What?" you say.

"The things you say," Allen says. "The things we say—how we say them sometimes."

"The things we say," you repeat.

"Like, why you said Lake Mead the way you said Lake Mead a few seconds ago," Allen says. "Stuff like that." He drinks some beer. "Who is making us say these things?"

You look at the sky.

"This lake, it brings back memories though," Allen says, and he points at the lake with the same hand he used before. "I guess it's a link to the past, for me."

Allen drinks some more beer.

•••

An hour passes.

You're still drinking the same beer.

You don't like the beer too much, you realize.

Allen is drinking #5.

He's a little tipsy, you think.

You notice there's a sunset happening.

'Get Free' by Major Lazer and Amber Coffman is playing

from inside the Chevy Malibu.

This is nice, you think.

You can actually see that the sun is moving too, when you squint, and it looks like the sun is falling, behind some low hills, in the distance.

You have never noticed this before and you don't really feel like telling Allen so you keep squinting.

Allen looks at you and then squints at something and laughs.

"They call this the magic hour—*golden hour*."

You look at Allen and say something.

"What?" Allen says.

"Who calls this the golden—magic hour?" And then you add his name, for emphasis. "Allen."

"It has to do with the lights and everything," Allen says, as he moves his arms in the air.

Then he points at something.

"Just look around at everything."

You look around at everything and you think you can make out the sound of the sun setting—or falling, you're not sure.

Things are getting strange, you think.

"No—things look just, more... more magical I guess, or something," Allen says. "In this light."

You make it look like you are looking around some more, just to satisfy Allen.

"The water looks really nice like this," Allen adds.

"Yeah," you say, looking like you are looking at the water,

or, at least, how you imagine you would look looking like you are looking at the water.

Then, you actually look at the water.

You don't say anything.

You peek—just for a second—at Allen.

He isn't even looking at the water.

Allen is crying about something.

BROWN HORSE IN BLUE WATER

That night, you have a recurring dream.

You're at Barry's place.

An apartment in the middle of the desert.

A meteor falls from the sky.

Nobody notices the meteor but you hear it hit—impact, somewhere off in the distance.

You feel the vibrations.

Barry says something to you but you don't listen.

An aging woman is walking around with a tray of appetizers.

James Franco looks happy.

He is talking to a bunch of actors you've never heard of.

"Luther," James Franco says to one of them.

There's a dead horse in the swimming pool.

"Who's the new guy?" someone says.

'Textes' by Mr. Oizo is playing.

The water makes little splashing noises every time the horse bumps into the side of the pool.

"Terrible things, at least he tries," someone says to James Franco.

It's balmy so you begin to sweat.

"Sometimes I like to press mute on the TV and just watch the images and do nothing," one of the actors says to another actor.

James Franco laughs.

"What's wrong with your face guy?" Barry says.

"My face," you say.

"Yeah, your face, guy," Barry says.

The pool makes the sound of water again as the horse bumps against the inside of the pool.

And you touch your face.

The phone rings and you wake up.

It's Barry.

You feel your face for growths.

"Where've you been?" Barry says.

"I was at your house—your apartment."

"My apartment?"

"In the middle of the desert."

"I don't live in the middle of the desert," Barry says. "Alton lives out in the desert."

"I don't know, it was a nightmare," you say. "Maybe."

You touch your face again, and feel for growths.

FANTASTIC PLANET

You call your mother.

"I found a new boyfriend," you say. "Some guy from Madrid."

That is how you describe your boyfriend.

You look out the window of your Manhattan triplex and then up at the Dodger blue sky.

Then you look at your walls.

You make up a name.

"Leonard."

You change your mind about the Madrid story.

"It's some guy from Manhattan, actually," you say. "Mom, sorry."

In Alaska, your mother is holding the phone in her left hand. She is wearing a Prada designer dress with a Gucci overcoat and some Nina Simone high-heels.

She is at a fancy restaurant and she is having dinner with the actor John Hurt.

She listens to you tell your lie about a boyfriend.

She looks down at the ground and then up at John Hurt (who smiles at her) and then after a while, down at her plate (she is eating salmon with a side of steamed potatoes), and she smiles a smile that was intended for you.

But John Hurt thinks the smile is for him so he smiles even harder.

She knows you are lying to her—your mother—but she doesn't say anything because she is having dinner with the actor John Hurt.

She doesn't say anything because she wants everything to be *normal*.

She wants to seem normal in front of John Hurt.

She doesn't want him to know about her problems.

She doesn't want things to change any.

So she just says, "Okay."

You look out the window of your Manhattan triplex.

You let out a sigh because the sky has now turned a faded cornflower blue.

And the walls no longer look the same white as last week's white.

More like a blotted out blue-white now.

MUSCLE MUSEUM

The middle part of 'Love on a Real Train' by Tangerine Dream is playing.

You call your dad.

"I found a new girlfriend," you say. "I met her at one of Ben Stiller's parties."

That is how you describe your new girlfriend.

You look out the window of your Manhattan triplex and up at the Yale blue sky and then at your walls.

You make up a name.

"Justine."

You change your mind about the Ben Stiller girlfriend story.

"I met her at a convention for disabled children in Peru, actually," you say, "father, sorry."

In Hawaii, your dad is holding the phone in his right hand. He is wearing a six-button Giorgio Armani three-piece suit, a Prada dress shirt, a burgundy Calvin Klein silk tie and leather Hugo Boss wing-tip shoes.

He is at home, alone.

He listens to you tell your lie about a girlfriend.

He looks up at the ceiling and then after a while, the ground.

He smiles and nods to himself because he loves you.

He knows you are lying to him—your dad—but he doesn't say anything because he also tells a lie.

"I've met someone, also," he says. "I'm dating again."

"I'm happy for you," you say, "that's great."

Again, you look out the window of your Manhattan triplex.

You let out a sigh because the sky has turned a powder blue-sort of blue.

The walls no longer look the same white as last week's white, in this light.

You say something else to your dad, then you hang up.

And then later—much later—you sit at a table and flip through a worn copy of *Palo Alto*.

You've never actually read the book—any of it—you realize.

So you open it and read 'Part I' of 'The Rainbow Goblins'.

•••

Your mind begins to wander.

James Franco is taking a bath.

You can hear it.

He is whistling 'Tango Passionata' by Pierro Umiliani.

IVY LEAGUE MUSIC

You give up on *Palo Alto*.

'Lower Your Eyelids to Die with the Sun' by M83 is playing from the stereo.

You read an article in issue 37 of *Music Scholars Quarterly*. It's about something called *Ivy League Music*.

The title reads 'Ivy League Music and our Conception of Time, Space and Moment in Relation to Music in the Post-Everything that is the Now'.

It's written by the woman you met at the party—from Minneapolis—who is having problems with her son who is in love with a boy from Lisbon.

Ryan.

You spend a good portion of twenty minutes reading the article. You find it interesting (actually) and highlight several passages.

"Ivy League Music is a music appreciated by students (and sometimes the staff) of the nation's most prestigious and affluent universities—and colleges" and "artists like Steve Reich, Ratatat, AraabMUZIK, Beck, Fuck Buttons, Sufjan Stevens, Rustie, Crystal Castles, Goblin, Tokyo Police

Club, Killer Mike, Devo, The Decemberists, The Libertines, Serge Gainsbourg, Radiohead, Nirvana, Janelle Monáe, Boards of Canada, David Lynch, Primus, Keyboard Kid 206, DJ Shadow, D'Angelo, Robyn, Jens Lekman, Ennio Morricone, Portishead, Gang Gang Dance, Gonjasufi, Kanye West, Slightly Stoppid, Sunn O))), The Books, Frank Zappa, Aphex Twin, Lil Wayne, El-P, Walt Mink, Broken Social Scene, Interpol, Girl Talk, Amon Tobin, Belle and Sebastian, The New Pornographers, Stereolab, The Wrens, Joanna Newsom, Nathan Fake, The National, The Fugees, The Shins, Justin Timberlake, Frank Ocean, Sun Ra, Simian Mobile Disco, J Dilla, Joy Orbison, Fleet Foxes, Otis Redding, Bruce Springsteen, Daft Punk, John Maus, Beach House, Madlib, Sbtrkt, LCD Soundsystem, DOOM, Jamie xx, OFWGKTA, Dirty Projectors, Elliott Smith, Bright Eyes, Sonic Youth, Japandroids, Arcade Fire, Del The Funky Homosapien, The Throne, The xx, tUnE-yArDs, Keep Shelly in Athens, Air, Bob Dylan, Fugazi, SebastiAn, Son Lux, Kyle Hall, The Weeknd, The Pains of Being Pure at Heart, St. Vincent, Nujabes, Jay-Z, Lana Del Rey, Modest Mouse, Outkast, James Blake, Rage Against the Machine, Optimus Rhyme, Mogwai, Deerhunter, Battles, Animal Collective (including, but not limited to: Terrestrial Tones, Vashti Bunyan, Together, etc.), Dan the Automator, Koreless, Pink Floyd, Skrillex, Wu-Tang Clan, Ariel Pink's Haunted Graffiti, Joy Division, The Streets, Destroyer, Gil Scott-Heron, Burial, Zomby, Neutral Milk Motel, James Pants, Girl Unit, A$AP Rocky, BNJMN, Trentemøller, Galaxie 500, Sigur Rós, Clams

Casino, French Fries, Jai Paul, Blawan, Rob Dougan, Spoon, RZA, Prince, R.E.M., Beastie Boys, Rick Ross, Bok Bok, Philip Glass, Actress, Washed Out, Vangelis, Dan Deacon, Vampire Weekend and others are a few of the more notable examples of this recent phenomenon that is Ivy League Music" and "Ivy League Music is a music that appeals to the predominately young crowd of intellectual and honored scholars"—basically any section with the words 'Ivy League Music,' you highlight.

'Mansard Roof' by Vampire Weekend begins to play.

MRS. GODZILLA

Kirsten Dunst comes over.

"I really liked *Palo Alto*," she says to James Franco, and then giggles. "I don't know if I told you already."

"Thanks," James Franco says.

Together—all three—you take turns doing drugs.

Different drugs.

You laugh a lot.

"This one makes you see music," Kirsten Dunst says to no one.

You tell stories of people you don't like.

You watch *The Life Aquatic with Steve Zissou* all the way through with no volume.

You overfeed the fish in the salt-water tank in the media room with the piano.

And then, you eat some chili—"Kirsten Dunst Style," Kirsten Dunst says (because this is what she likes to call it whenever she makes chili, you understand).

•••

Eventually, you're all lying on the floor, in the living room.

The carpet smells of feet and food and shoes and cleaning.

You think about the moon and living on the moon.

"Don't you think it'd be like, amazing to live up there?" you say to no one in particular.

"Live up where?" Kirsten Dunst says to James Franco.

"I don't know, I didn't say it," James Franco says to Kirsten Dunst and then laughs and looks at you.

"Like up there," you say, pointing at the ceiling. "The moon."

"Oh, the moon," Kirsten Dunst says.

"No one lives on the moon," James Franco says quietly.

"Yeah, that," Kirsten Dunst says, "who knows?"

You do some more drugs.

"So what does it actually feel like?" you say.

"Which one?" Kirsten Dunst says.

This time, she actually sounds somewhat intrigued by the vagueness of your question.

She is also petting James Franco's hair.

You point to a pastel baggie—orange—on the floor.

"The mushrooms," you say.

"The mushrooms," Kirsten Dunst says. "Well, this one time I took them with Salma Hayek and, you know the part in the Matthew Broderick version of *Godzilla*, when Godzilla attacks the city and like steps on all the people?" Kirsten Dunst says.

You nod.

"Like in the very beginning, when that old fisherman

nearly gets killed on the pier?"

"Yeah, but—no—I thought you said the part where she attacks the city and starts stepping on people?"

"Well yeah, that, but then the part where the fisherman nearly gets killed on the pier?" Kirsten Dunst says.

"Okay."

"Yeah—well, it feels like that."

"Which part?"

"Hmm?"

"The part on the pier," James Franco says.

"Like, what do you mean?" you say.

James Franco makes a comment about how you sound genuinely concerned about the specificity of Kirsten Dunst's statement.

You ask again.

"Which part does it feel like?"

"Like, it feels like Godzilla is literally attacking the city," she says.

You contemplate something and then say, "That doesn't sound like much fun."

"Oh but it is—especially if you do it with a friend," she says.

•••

Five minutes pass.

Nobody says anything.

"So Salma Hayek is your friend?" you say.

"No, not really," Kirsten Dunst says.

•••

Kirsten Dunst rolls a joint.

"You can't know if you don't try," James Franco says.

The Life Aquatic with Steve Zissou is on again.

You are watching a scene with Willem Dafoe.

He is screaming something at Bill Murray.

The stereo is on, also. It's faint but you can hear it now.

'The Great Escape' by Moby is playing.

You close your eyes.

James Franco says something.

You don't pay attention.

Kelli Scarr sings.

...just to watch you perform the great escape. I'll pull your arms tight behind your back.

BUK-KAKE

Barry calls to tell you about a party.

"There's a party," Barry says. "Tonight."

"There's a party tonight?" you say. "Where is there a party tonight?"

"There's a party in Laurel Canyon tonight," Barry says.

"Tonight?"

"I'll come pick you up later."

"Who lives in Laurel Canyon?" you say.

"Which car should I take?"

You repeat the question.

"Kirk lives in Laurel Canyon."

"Who's Kirk?"

"Kirk is the guy who lives in Laurel Canyon," Barry says.

•••

In Laurel Canyon, it's hot outside.

There are hills and mansions and tennis courts and swimming pools and palm trees and tiki torches.

Everything you expected.

At the party, people are wearing masks.

"You didn't tell me this was going to be a costume party,"

you say to Barry.

"No one told me this was going to be a costume party," Barry says.

You sigh.

One guy—the mask he is wearing—looks a little like Stanley Kubrick.

It's the only mask you recognize.

One girl, you think her mask looks like Amy Winehouse but you don't feel like talking so you do nothing.

You talk to Barry instead.

•••

An hour passes.

And then it's a little after eleven and your yawning becomes more noticeable.

"Stop yawning so much," Barry says.

"Stop standing by me so much," you say.

On the stereo: 'Stars Are Blind' by Paris Hilton.

A group of people arrive to the party—late.

Very late.

"Because it's late to be fashionable," one of them says.

She said it wrong, you think.

And then another one, a girl, she says, "Dork."

They are all laughing and drinking Patrón and Hennessey and wearing masks.

At the party, you spot: Debra, because of the enormous engagement ring she is wearing ("a gift from Japanese art house film director Harold Yen" she once explained); Julius, because he is the only black person at the party; Teddy

Hoover, because of his extremely well-groomed beard—a curious bump under the mask; Edward Price, because of the expensive and extremely crisp Prada three-piece suit; Evian Day, because of his affinity for the color purple and the fact that he is also bald; Fabio, the long blond hair and expensive perfume; one of the super models from another party earlier in the month: tattoo of a jaguar on her left arm; the three waiters again, in uniform; that one exec from the other party, a little shorter than last time it seems; and Marques sans mask.

And then Kirk, obviously.

On the stereo, Julian Casablancas croons.

...I've got nothing to say, I've got nothing to say, I've got nothing to say, I'm in utter dismay I've got nothing to say.

You step outside and smoke a cigarette.

You notice the Hollywood hills and the several mansions and the two tennis courts and the one swimming pool and the numerous palm trees and the various tiki torches and the hot tub and the green house and the tool shed and a couple of black stretch limos and one white limo and a Jaguar XJ and a Rolls-Royce Phantom Coupé and a Bentley Continental GT and a Ferrari and a Maserati Kubang and a basketball court (which you failed to notice the first time) and some lawn chairs and an enormous golf course and a few modern lawn sculptures and a giant fountain with a statue of JFK and a road sign that reads *dead end*.

You look back inside, at the people.

'I Would Die 4 U' by Prince And The Revolution is

playing.

Everything begins to smell of smoke.

You hate it so you put out the cigarette.

You wonder if you have any Mentos.

You check your pockets—all of them—for Mentos.

You don't have any Mentos.

You go back inside and look for Barry.

The party lasts another two hours, maybe.

RYAN GOSLING

You're at a screening.

The film is about a man who is forced to work for someone he doesn't like.

And later, the man realizes he is maybe telepathic, or telekinetic, you forget.

During one of the sad scenes, a song you recognize plays: 'Born To Die' by Lana Del Rey.

The film lasts two hours, maybe.

After it's over, you spot someone.

He looks a lot like Ryan Gosling.

Maybe it is Ryan Gosling, you think.

You hide.

You sit with Tori Spelling and someone else.

"I was on Oprah," someone says.

You hide for a few minutes longer.

Suddenly, you are bored with everything. Tori Spelling is talking about a film. It's not very interesting—what she has to say so you get up and leave.

You see Ryan Gosling again, this time from far away.

His back is facing you.

That's not Ryan Gosling, you realize.
Someone else.
George Clooney maybe.
No.
Brad Pitt.

MAMMOTH LAKE

Something on the television makes the sound of birds in the sky.

"I want to tell you about Mammoth Lake," Barry says.

"Mammoth Lakes?" you say.

The woman on the television says something about Miami.

"No, Mammoth Lake," Barry says. "Without the '*s*' at the end."

The television makes the sound of birds in the sky, again.

"Have you ever been to Mammoth Lake?"

"No," you say

You both sit in silence for a while.

Barry looks at the television screen.

He says something.

A man is talking about the weather.

You say something about Lake Mead, and Allen.

Barry looks at you.

He doesn't say anything.

And then, "I've never told you about Mammoth Lake?"

You think *Mammoth Lake* and then you look at Barry.

"No, you've never told me about Mammoth Lake," you say.

On the television: a commercial for cars.

Nissan.

"Remind me later to tell you about Mammoth Lake then," Barry says.

You say something and you nod but Barry doesn't see this because he is looking at the television, and the cars, and he is laughing because the commercial is funny.

BED AND A FUNERAL

You wake up in the middle of the night.

You think maybe that you wet the bed.

You look down and feel the bed.

You don't see anything.

You can't see anything.

You turn on the lights.

You feel again for wetness.

The bed is dry.

The phone rings.

It's your father.

He tells you your grandmother—his mother—is dead.

"She passed away," he says.

"How did it happen?" you say.

"She died in her sleep I think," your father says.

"That's safe," you say.

"It's safe, yeah," your father says.

•••

You fly to Ireland, for the funeral.

You go with your father, James Franco and your mother.

You meet some of the extended family and they ask you a

lot of questions.

Like: "Is James Franco a boyfriend?"

James Franco smiles because the question is funny.

And then someone asks something else, a cousin maybe.

"You should see him in *Spiderman 3*," you say.

AMERICAN JUSTICE

You drive to Hardees because you want a hamburger.

It's late afternoon.

Inside Hardees, Justice is eating.

Also, there are people taking pictures, from outside.

Lots of pictures.

There is a sign that reads: *What would happen if a Thickburger jumped into a cold swimming pool?* And then at the bottom, after a picture of a Thickburger in swimming shorts, the word: *Shrinkage.*

A lot of people in the restaurant are just standing around. They aren't even ordering food. They're just staring at Justice.

Gaspard Augé and Xavier de Rosnay are both eating a Monster Thickburger and a Muzak version of 'Corfu' by Eric Gemsa is playing.

No one notices you.

They probably don't realize it's you.

Whatever.

You order something.

Someone says something about London and then some

kid with red hair says, "Dude Frank, Daft Punk."

Someone from behind the counter hands you a Thickburger.

You walk past the crowd and open the door and walk out to the parking lot.

You get into the Ferrari.

It takes a minute, but you find it.

You press play.

'Veridis Quo' by Daft Punk begins to play.

It settles in.

You think about it.

Then you look out the window into the Hardees and stare (hard) at Gaspard Augé and Xavier de Rosnay.

ANDY WARHOL HOUSE

You watch *Bio-Dome*.

You dance to 'My Drive Thru' by Pharrell Williams and Santigold and Julian Casablancas.

An hour passes.

You call Gwyneth Paltrow.

It's a little before eight.

She picks up.

She listens.

You tell her you need to talk to someone and she tells you it's fine so you talk.

You talk about books, humidifiers, white walls, typewriters, Channing Tatum, mineral oil, vitamin pills, a mountain in Japan, Steve Harvey, air fresheners, something Uma Thurman said last week, toxic waste, European cows, Twitter, Japanese music, Old Navy and Kenneth Cole shoes.

After a while—five minutes—you tell her you need to talk in person.

She says this is fine—also.

You drive the Bentley to Gwyneth Paltrow's house.

On the way down, you listen to 'Under Control' by The Strokes.

You find the house.

The house is somewhere in the middle of the suburbs.

Inside the house, you can see that things are being moved around.

She's remodeling the house.

You say something about carpet designs from around the world and coffee table books.

"Oh, like the Andy Warhol coffee table book," Gwyneth Paltrow says.

"What Andy Warhol coffee table book?" you say.

"*The* Andy Warhol coffee table book," she says again.

You stare at her.

She stands up and leaves the room.

'Such Great Heights' by The Postal Service is playing from somewhere.

Two minutes pass.

Gwyneth Paltrow returns with a book.

She sets it down on the coffee table and you pick it up.

The Coffee Table Andy Warhol Picture Book.

You flip through some of the pages, for about ten seconds and then you ask Gwyneth Paltrow something.

"That's because we have two coffee tables," she says.

ENTOURAGE

It's early morning.

You are tired of listening to 'Maps' by Yeah Yeah Yeahs so you turn off the radio.

You say James Franco's name but he does not come.

This is because he is out having brunch with Cameron Diaz.

He left a note on the refrigerator—to explain all of this—but you don't see it.

You get angry, and this lasts for maybe three days.

On the fourth day, you're sorry, so you apologize.

You say, "James Franco, I'm sorry."

"It's okay," James Franco says.

"I'm an idiot sometimes."

"It's okay," James Franco says. "You're fine. I forgive you."

And together, you listen to Vampire Weekend.

Different songs, all weekend, in no particular order.

"I think 'Mansard Roof' might be their best song," James Franco says.

BRUCE WILLIS IS DEAD

"My name is Bruce Willis," Bruce Willis says.

'Diplomat's Son' by Vampire Weekend is playing from somewhere inside the house.

You make a comment about the weather and then say something like "Bruce Willis is a pretty unusual name for someone who isn't actually Bruce Willis."

And Bruce Willis says, "Yeah, I guess."

You laugh about this and Bruce Willis mentions that he is from somewhere in the Midwest.

You talk about his education.

"Princeton for three years," Bruce Willis says. "Then I dropped out."

"Because it was too hard?" you say.

"My father died," Bruce Willis says. "Someone needed to support my mother."

"Middle child?" you say.

"Only child," Bruce Willis says.

"Oh."

You show Bruce Willis to his room.

"This is your room," you say.

Bruce Willis walks into the room.

He checks everything and then—for some reason—looks under the mattress.

"There's something here," Bruce Willis says.

This wasn't supposed to happen until much later.

You pretend.

"There's something where?"

You know exactly what's there because you put it there.

Bruce Willis shows you an envelope.

A stash.

Pictures and Polaroids.

You look at the pictures.

You took them—well, most of them.

There are: mountains in Africa, golf courses in Italy, Greek mythological creatures, clouds in a Peruvian sky, swimming pools in France, abandoned piano factories in Germany, solar eclipses from around the world, various animals in captivity—cages, Brazilian jungles, Egyptian pyramids, Hindu gods, and then, naked pictures of things.

Areolas, anuses, vulvae, scrota, cocks.

People too.

Celebrities.

One of Angelina Jolie, one of Scarlett Johansson, one of Jake Gyllenhaal, one of Charlize Theron (or at least someone who looks a lot like Charlize Theron—you didn't take that picture), three of Britney Spears at different ages, one badly photoshopped image of Sylvester Stallone holding his cock and a black and white of David Beckham on a bed, covered in some kind of jelly.

"Is it alright if I call you Willis?" you ask.

"Willis is fine," Bruce Willis says.

"Okay. Keep the photos, Willis," you say.

"Very good sir," Bruce Willis says.

You pat Bruce Willis on the shoulder and leave the room.

Bruce Willis returns the images to the brown manila envelope and then to the mattress under which they lay.

He smiles to himself because he is especially pleased with the Sylvester Stallone picture—he finds it to be rather exceptional.

'Arrow' by Vampire Weekend begins to play all throughout the house.

ARTIFACTS

There's an email from Barry.

A message and then, an attachment.

This is Eric, the message reads.

Eric.avi is the name for the attachment.

You open the file.

At first, you can't believe it.

It's a porno. Nothing expensive though.

The video looks super grainy and full of artifacts, like it was shot on a cell phone.

The video is post-marked 2006.

'Venus' by Logic System is playing on iTunes.

In the video, a man enters Eric from behind.

After a few seconds, the man pulls out and tells Eric to lie down.

Eric lies flat on his stomach and a second man walks in, from the right.

He puts his penis in Eric's mouth and Eric pleasures the man.

The other one, the first man, he watches, as Eric and the second man do things for a while.

Off-screen, someone says something to Eric.

Eric stops pleasuring the man and looks into the camera.

He stands up as the second man begins to masturbate.

The second man then ejaculates onto Eric's stomach.

The first man, he bends over and offers himself to Eric.

Eric mounts the man.

After a bit, Eric loses his erection and pulls out.

The second man walks over and helps Eric.

He tugs at the penis, violently, and then puts it in his mouth.

Eric sits back on the bed.

After a bit, he is hard again.

The first man, he is standing off to one side of the room and he is stroking himself.

Then, he walks over and urinates all over Eric and the second man.

This is the last part.

APPARTCHIK

You are at a party.

On the wall, there are paintings of mountains and blue skies and cars—dozens of them.

In the hallway, there is a woman in a gold dress speaking to someone on her iPhone.

She is talking about some new film that just came out.

You watch her—not because she is especially beautiful or anything—because something about her attracts you.

She does—has something.

You realize *it's the way she walks*, back and forth, as she is talking. That's why you keep watching her—why you think she is so interesting.

Everything she does—is so... elegant.

You think about Mt. Fuji and you look at the paintings to see if you can't maybe spot Mt. Fuji.

And then you are interrupted.

"I'm Ken," someone says from behind you.

You turn around.

"Nice to meet you, I don't believe we've ever met," Ken says.

Ken is an extraordinary man in a plain white suit.

He extends his arm.

You think about blond hair.

Ken's hair is brown.

You remember Clive—or Clyde, you can't remember.

"Hi," you say, and extend your arm, also.

You accept the handshake—a deceptively firm handshake.

"We might have spoken before," Ken says, as he returns his right hand to his right pants pocket. "In passing maybe."

"That is a possibility," you say.

'God Shuffled His Feet' by Crash Test Dummies is playing.

"I hear you like Vampire Weekend," he says.

You nod.

"Yes."

"And I hear you are friends with a certain James Franco," he says.

Again, you nod.

"James Franco was my roommate," he smiles, "Columbia."

You nod.

"Good book," he says. "*Palo Alto*."

"Yes, good book," you say.

You think about Nosferatu for some reason.

And then you raise your glass.

You notice it is empty.

KALAHARI

You drive the Ferrari across the desert.

The sand is red and there are no lakes.

'Classy Penguin' by The Books is playing.

"You're like super sweaty," James Franco says.

"I'm like, super fucking sweaty always," you say. "What desert is this?"

"I'm not sure," James Franco says.

"Call Barry."

"Why should I call Barry?" James Franco says.

"Just call Barry."

"No, why should I call Barry?"

"Because he'll know."

"He'll know what?"

"He'll know what desert we're on," you say.

"I'm not calling Barry to ask him what desert we're on," James Franco says.

You look out the driver's window.

"I think this is the Kalahari desert."

James Franco doesn't laugh.

Instead, he says, "What's the deal with Barry anyway?"

"How do you mean?"

"What is his purpose in life?"

"His job? Business *stuff*," you say.

"And?"

"And his deal is that he does business stuff. I don't know what else to tell you James Franco. Honestly, what do you want me to say? What is this? Why are you doing this? Why here? Why *now*?"

"I don't know," James Franco says. "Things."

He looks out the passenger side window of the Ferrari.

And then he says, "I just don't like Barry, I think, is all."

•••

Several hours pass.

You're driving the Ferrari across the desert again, back into the city this time.

Outside, it's dark.

Silence.

•••

An hour passes.

James Franco says something, out of nowhere.

This is the first thing he's said in nine hours.

You pay attention.

"What do you think happens in movies?" James Franco says. "Like, after everything's over."

"The movies?" you say.

"Characters," James Franco says. "What happens to them?"

"Characters in a movie?"

"Yeah, characters in a movie—film," James Franco says, "after the film's over, and it's done, what happens to them?"

You say something and James Franco interrupts you.

"My point is, I guess—have you ever thought about that, at all, like: the characters? Where characters go after a movie is over?"

You think about this and James Franco says something else but you don't pay attention because you are thinking about what he just said about movies and characters and you tell him to stop interrupting you.

He stops talking.

You say something vague about movies and their characters.

"No, not like that," James Franco says.

"Well then I have never given it serious thought, no, James Franco, I guess," you say, eventually, pissed, and look over at him.

James Franco sighs and slouches back into his seat.

"Nevermind," James Franco says.

Minutes pass.

"I met Ken," you say.

"Oh yeah?"

"Yeah."

James Franco looks out the passenger side window and doesn't say anything.

Now he is super-sweaty.

"Nevermind," you say.

'Sleep Walk' by Santo & Johnny is playing.

SUPERHERO PARTY

There's a party.

Everyone is dressed as a superhero.

The idea is that the costume, or superhero, needs to end in *man* or at least have the word in the title.

It's everyone you've ever known, at the party, for the most part.

Some of the costumes stand out, more than the others.

Spiderwoman is Celine Dione (she organized everything).

Superman is Barry.

You're Batman.

Scott, the astrophysicist, is Aquaman.

James Franco is Plastic Man.

Aron is Animal Man.

Christian is Wonder Man.

Tyrone is Meteor Man.

Marques is Amazing Man.

Juliette is Sandman.

Dezzy is Hawkman.

Manuel is Iron Man.

Teddy Hoover is the Human Bomb.

Some of the costumes look ridiculous too (like Aquaman and Iron Man and Animal Man) but everyone is drinking and people are laughing.

•••

Later.

Something in the house makes the sound of books falling from a bookshelf. Spiderwoman looks at Superman and Aquaman looks at Iron Man, who looks at Amazing Man.

"Books just fell from a shelf, I think," Spiderwoman says.

"I'll check it out," Plastic Man says.

"No, it's fine," you say. "It's probably just the wind."

Plastic Man stands up and looks at you.

Superman stares at you.

Meteor Man doesn't say anything.

"You're drunk," Superman says. "There is no wind."

"Who's drunk?" you say to Superman.

"You're drunk," Aquaman says.

You turn your head and look at Aquaman.

"I'm drunk?" you say to Aquaman.

"Yes, you're drunk," Hawkman says.

"Not this again," Martian Manhunter says.

You turn to look at Martian Manhunter.

Martian Manhunter is Bruce Willis

"What's going on?" Sandman says.

You stand up.

"Where is he going?" Amazing Man says.

'Tonight We are Young' by fun. is playing.

"Not what again?" Spiderwoman says.

"You're drunk," Superman says, again.

"Okay," you say to Superman, "I'm drunk."

"Sit down," Iron Man says.

You feel defeated so you sit.

"I'm gonna go check on the noise," Plastic Man says.

No one says anything.

Plastic Man leaves the room.

Jack Nicholson is out in the hallway.

He's dressed as Wolverine and he's talking to Wonder Woman: the supermodel from the costume party in Laurel Canyon, with the tattoo of the jaguar on her left arm.

Wolverine says *hi* to Plastic Man.

THE DOUBLE FEATURE

You watch a film.

Something about the end of the world.

It's a long film but you have time.

Basically, it's about the world and society—how everything functions, how things work.

The film opens with the world ending, just like that.

It's quick too.

There's a Rapture, but it's quick.

God makes an appearance.

God is a man in a white robe.

White beard too.

Generic shit.

He says some things about the world ending.

You find out, later, that God lives on the moon, actually.

In the film, the moon is Heaven and Hell is really a volcano in South America.

All the good people went to live on the moon.

Satan doesn't show for the Rapture though.

In fact, nobody knows where he is.

Many people are left behind—mostly those of the 1%.

The movie lasts three hours, maybe.

At one point, there is a zombie apocalypse, a second and third coming, the unveiling of the anti-Christ, several alien invasions (the aliens lived at the bottom of the sea it turns out), the appearance of some sort of leviathan in the Pacific and then the eventual disappearance of Big Foot.

There is a scene with Tom Hanks.

More like a cameo.

The film has a sad ending.

The main character—Jake Gyllenhaal—perishes, dies, on top of a mountain.

Or, falls into a volcano rather—in Europe.

You remember the title of the film: *Mastodon Farm*.

And you remember liking it, a lot.

•••

You watch another film.

This one opens with a purple screen.

'It's A Sin' by Pet Shop Boys begins to play.

The opening credits—white letters on a purple background.

Actors you've never heard of.

Then the title screen: *Brown Horse in Blue Water*.

The purple fades, slowly, and reveals a man staring into the camera. A Japanese man, or, at least of Asian descent. He is grinning and he is wearing a name tag.

It reads: 'Hello, my name is: Mr. Grin'.

From off-screen, the Japanese slash Asian man grabs a camera. A Pentax DSLR and begins to laugh, loudly.

He takes a picture of the audience—us, you—and then there is a flash.

Images begin to flood the screen.

A man in the desert.

Mt. Kilimanjaro melting.

David Hasselhoff and Toby Maguire having sex.

Steven Segal jumping from out of a helicopter into the North Atlantic.

Whoopi Goldberg in the middle of a corn field—skeet shooting.

Jamie Lee Curtis checking her toilet paper for blood.

And then, 'Safe' by Atticus Ross begins to play.

In one review, a critic applauds the film for having *courage.*

"It doesn't matter if their actions don't make sense. All characters exist, in some sense, to operate in the world they were created in. They make their own decisions. It is our job to try and figure out what they mean, or don't."

In one scene, Kevin Bacon opens a door and music begins to play.

This film, you don't like—not so much.

COCONUT GROVE

You drive to Coconut Grove.

It's four in the morning and you are thinking about palm trees and lakes and waterfalls and mountains.

You listen to 'Please Forgive My Heart' by Bobby Womack.

It takes a while—a couple of hours actually—but, you get to Coconut Grove, eventually.

In Coconut Grove, you own a beach house.

The beach house, it belonged to Mark Ruffalo—back in late 2006.

You read something by Henry Miller and 'Mirages' by Sabrina Ratté & Le Révélateur is playing. And somehow, even with all of this happening, you fall asleep.

You wake up, a few hours later.

You feel exhausted, still, but you get out of bed.

You walk over to one of the three bathrooms and look at yourself in the full-body mirror.

I look like shit you think.

You rub your eyes and climb back into bed.

You sleep, again. This time for nine hours.

You have dreams, several dreams.

You dream you are falling in space.

You dream of sand turning to glass.

You dream you are a bear with growths on your face.

You dream of the Nile.

You dream of something exploding inside your body.

You dream you are happily married.

And then, pictures—images of planets, outer space, collisions, accidents and fender-benders. Squid guts, everywhere.

You dream of volcanoes in Italy and ocean water in Jamaica and mammoth fish in Japan.

And then you dream of space, again—the same dream as before.

You are alone and you are falling and you are naked.

But it's like you are floating.

The song 'Oh My Love' by Riz Ortolani and Katyna Ranieri is playing from somewhere.

You can see the moon is some sort of pale lavender, instead of the typical grey-blue you know.

And you notice, also, that there are people on the moon. Lots of people, actually.

They are wearing African masks and they are waving at you.

And you wonder, *are these people actually living on the moon?*

They are saying things but you cannot hear them because you are falling through space.

Everything is black, and cold and quiet and you feel no wind.

They look like toys—the people—you think, little miniature toys. The kind you would find in a dollhouse.

And as you are falling, everything is moving in super slow motion; the birds, too.

Those, you can hear.

You fall some more and then things just sort of start to fade to grey.

And you scream, because you are scared, but no one can hear you because you are in space.

You look at the birds, and you keep screaming.

•••

The following day, the stereo is on but nothing is playing.

You go outside and smoke a cigarette.

You suck on a Mentos at the same time.

Everything is super bright.

The air is brisk—*crisp*, you think.

And the moon is gone now.

You walk out to the pier.

Someone recognizes you.

They say something and you wave.

You think about life on other planets.

Someone once said: "There are things you wouldn't believe—up there—things you couldn't even begin to imagine."

An hour later, you are all alone.

Those people who recognized you, they're gone, also.

Barry once said, "You never smile."
You think about this.
There's no one to direct this segment.
You look up into the sky.
It's *bright*.
You don't see anything.
You can't see anything.
The sun, you think.

ACKNOWLEDGEMENTS

Super important thanks to Johnny Buse and Christian Caminiti.

And I can't forget Mario Macías, Lawrence Sumulong, Mark Sullivan, Nkemdirim Offor and Andrew Lippman.

Also, Isabelle Zapata, Andrea Kalocai and Santiago Guedán.

A genuine "you're awesome," to a very special group of professors. Susan Ireland, David Harrison, Kesho Scott, Heather Lobban-Viravong, Katya Gibel-Mevorach, Lakesia Johnson, Theresa Geller, Jeremy Jackson, John Domini and Ralph Savarese.

Et un grand merci à Monique Teghillo, Sylvie De Vito, Gwen Curt, Célia Janin-Thivos *et* Annick Chabanon.

Andersen Prunty, for working with me and being totally *Zen* about everything! Thank you.

Totally indebted to this group: Ken Sparling, Noah Cicero, (Professor) D. Harlan Wilson, Cameron Pierce, Sam Pink, Nick Antosca and Bradley Sands.

Others who also helped: Ofelia Hunt, J. David Osborne, Jordan Krall, Josh Myers and Lil Jabba.

Love you: Grinnell College, the country of France, the Internet and the Midwest.

A very special and heartfelt thanks to Nana & Fritz Bingel. *Grüß dich,* Karolin!

And of course, thank you to my mother and father.

Mike Kleine was born in December of 1988. He graduated from Grinnell College with a B.A. in French literature. Someday, he will begin his M.A. in English literature. He currently lives somewhere in the Midwest. This is his first book.

CPSIA information can be obtained at www.ICGtesting.com
Printed in the USA
BVOW082015041012

302196BV00001B/4/P